Hornet

by

Chris Powling

Illustrated by Alan Marks

First published in 2009 in Great Britain by
Barrington Stoke Ltd
18 Walker St, Edinburgh, EH3 7LP

www.barringtonstoke.co.uk

ISBN: 978-1-84299-647-8

Printed in Great Britain by Bell & Bain Ltd

A Note from the Author

I've always loved stories about the wild west of America more than a hundred years ago. In those days you had to be a hero just to stay alive. That's if you did stay alive. I hope *Hornet* keeps you guessing about Gil, Molly and their father right to the end.

For
The Wild Bunch
(Jake, Polly and Suzie)

Contents

Chapter 1
The Visitor

Sunrise is a good time for a killer. There are long shadows to hide in. And the world is still waking up. That's all the help he needs to put you in your coffin.

So maybe Gil should have seen this coming. He took a step away from the water tub. He wiped the soap from his face. He felt around for his glasses. "Why the gun, mister?" he asked.

The visitor patted his horse's neck. "The gun, kid?" he said. "Oh ... you mean this gun. The gun I'm stickin' in your face. I'm glad you can see it and that's a fact. Can't be easy seein' anythin' with specs as thick as yours are."

"I can see pretty good, mister."

"Not for shootin' a gun, you can't. Or so they told me back in town. Without those specs you're as blind as a bat. Must have broke your old Pa's heart – him bein' sheriff an' all. Also him bein' just about the best shot in the county."

"Leave Pa out of it, OK?"

The visitor sat back in the saddle. "OK by me, kid," he said. "Seeing your Pa is as dead as that there water in the tub. Killed by some hoodlum, wasn't he?"

"Shot in the back," said Gil.

"In the back, eh? The hoodlum must've been usin' the brains God gave him ... your Pa bein' such a hot shot. Still, it's saved me a bit of bother."

"Has it?"

"You bet it has," the visitor said. "It's saved me the bother of shooting your Pa myself."

And suddenly he smiled.

It was a nasty smile. Gil could see that even without his glasses. It was the sort of smile a killer wears when he's about to put you in your coffin.

Chapter 2

Payback Time

Gil looked up at the man on horseback.

"Who are you, mister?" he asked.

"Name's Hornet."

"Hornet?"

"James Elroy Hornet. Like the nasty little critter that stings you so bad. I do a bit of stingin' myself, to tell the truth. That's if someone owes me … and your Pa owed me big-time."

"Owed you for what?"

"For ten years in jail, kid. Ten stinkin' years I'll never get back. Just for stealing a couple of his steers. Cattle-rustling, he called it – then he beat me to the draw with that fancy gun play of his. And now he's gone and died on me. So someone else has got to pay. Maybe someone like you."

Hornet's eyes flashed. The gun in his hand didn't move. He looked round the trim, tidy yard. "Now this place should do it," he said. "A handy little property on a bend in the river? Must be worth ten years of anyone's life ..."

"You want our ranch?"

"My ranch from tomorrow. Call it payback from your Pa. I'll be here at sunrise with the papers."

Coolly, Hornet bent forward. He lifted the glasses from Gil's nose and tossed them high in the air. Just before they fell, he fired a single shot.

CRACK!

The glasses vanished in a spatter of glass. "There now," said Hornet with an evil grin. "That look on your face made me jumpy.

I always want to sting something when I'm jumpy."

He slid the gun back in its holster. "Till tomorrow then," he said. "I'll bring some pals if that's OK with you. Get your sister to fix us some breakfast."

"Do we have any choice?"

"Shame on you, kid. You've always got a choice. This time it's between livin' and dyin'."

Hornet raised his hat in a polite way. He took his time about leaving. At all four fences in the yard he got off his horse and ran his fingers over the woodwork. He checked every plank, every post and every gate. "Neat as a new pin, kid," he called. "That Pa of yours would be real proud of you and your sister."

It was as if the ranch was already his.

Chapter 3

Bad Omen

Gil had forgotten how the deep ruts and loose rocks made the wagon bounce all over the trail. He'd forgotten the dust as well. It rose behind them like a cloud – a choking, yellow cloud without a drop of water. "I've spent too long at college back East," he said.

"It's what Pa wanted," said Molly. "It was one of his dreams, Gil – a doctor in the family."

"I'm not a doctor yet, sis."

"But you will be very soon. Another year at college and you'll have passed all your exams."

"If I ever get back to college."

"Hornet, you mean?"

"He's a true-born killer, Molly. And he thinks it's payback time. Pa's dead and gone. So who is there left in town to stop him and his so-called pals?"

"Our own pals," Molly said.

"You reckon?"

"Let's give them a chance, Gil. Let's give ourselves a chance as well. Isn't that how Pa would play it?"

Molly pulled the wagon to a stop under an old elm tree that hung over the trail. "Look back," she said. "Every inch of this land is ours, Gil. From here all the way to the foot hills. Pa cleared it with his own hands. Then he built the yard and the ranch-house for when he retired. Isn't that worth fighting for?"

Gil said nothing.

Molly gave him a sharp look. He was gazing into the elm tree. Something was hanging up there in its branches – something grey and wispy, a big sack-like thing. It was like a huge fruit that might fall at any moment. And it made an odd noise. The sound was like a soft buzz. "Nasty little critters," Gil said. "They'll sting you if they get jumpy. Did Hornet bring that nest with him, sis?"

Chapter 4

A Reminder

Bad news travels fast. The whole town knew why they'd come. Gil and Molly saw it in every face – how people blinked and frowned and looked away fast.

At least Molly saw it. All Gil saw without his glasses was a dim blur. But he knew what was going on. "They're afraid," he said. He sounded bitter. "They're afraid we'll stop and ask them for help."

"You can blame Pa for that," said Molly.

"Pa?"

"He did all the brave stuff for them, Gil. For years and years. In the end they forgot how to be brave themselves."

"So why have we bothered to come here?"

"Maybe to remind them."

She gave a tug at the horse's reins. The wagon stopped in front of a long, low cabin built of pale old wood. There was nothing smart or fancy about it. It looked as simple and solid as a strong box. Over the main door hung a sign. In clear, bold letters this said: COUNTY JAIL.

Molly let go of the horse's reins but stayed in her seat on the wagon. "Then again ..." she went on.

"Yes?"

"... maybe we came to remind ourselves."

She was looking hard at the jail house as she said this. There, under the sun porch, three men were slumped in rocking chairs. Two of them were dozing. The third one wasn't. James Elroy Hornet was the kind of true-born killer who never dozes.

Chapter 5

Some Like Them Soft

Hornet poked the men on either side of him. "Now, ain't this dandy?" he said. "We got company, boys."

All three of them rose to their feet. They were so alike they could have been triplets. They had the same trail-dusty boots and shirts, the same wide-brimmed hats, the same guns hanging snug and low on their hips. But most of all they had the same eyes ... hard, cold eyes that missed nothing.

Molly smiled in a polite manner. "Good day to you, Mr Hornet," she said. "I hear you're coming to breakfast tomorrow."

"Softly done, ma'am."

"What?"

"My eggs," said Hornet. "Theirs, too."

"Softly done it is, then," Molly said. "Funny that … I had you down for hard-boiled guys not softies."

"Are you joshing with me, little lady?"

"I wouldn't dream of it, Mr Hornet. Not if it makes you jumpy. We've already seen what happens when you're jumpy. Other people's property gets shot to bits."

Molly clucked at the horse who set off at a trot. The wagon swung back across the street till it faced the way they'd come.

Everyone in town was watching as Gil and Molly left for home. But no one said a word. It was as if the three men on the porch had gagged every one of them.

Chapter 6

Target Practice

Inside the barn there was the crack of gunshots. Gil checked the target he'd pinned to a wall. So far, he'd fired more than a hundred bullets. And so far he'd hit the target twice. "I need my glasses, Molly!" he moaned.

"Gil, that's hog-wash!" said his sister. "With or without glasses, you've always been hopeless with guns. Pa never cared about that. He wanted you to save lives not take them. That's why he sent you to college to become a doctor."

"Pa isn't here any more, Molly. But James Elroy Hornet is ... and he'll be here at sunrise tomorrow. The brave stuff is down to us now. You said that yourself."

"Not just down to us, Gil!"

"Who else is there?"

"Everyone we know, that's who. OK, so Hornet and his gang may try to grab our ranch. But how long will they keep it? Do you think Pa's friends will just let it happen?"

"Yes," said Gil. "I do."

"All they need is a bit of time, Gil ..."

Molly broke off. She knew it was no good talking to Gil. Her brother was lifting his gun again. She saw his finger squeeze the trigger. She saw the flash, sniffed the smoke and heard the bullet strike home – in this case deep in the barn roof. The shot was so far off target it was almost funny. But Molly didn't laugh.

She didn't dare.

They were too close to sunrise for that.

Chapter 7

Showdown

It was as cold as a dead man's kiss. The top of the hills glinted with the gold of sunrise. Far below, the world still lay in shadow. Gil could only just see the old elm tree up ahead of him. Its branches hung over the trail like a tall, wide arch leading onto

the land Pa had got for when he retired. No,
it was their land now – his and Molly's.

But maybe not for long.

Gil felt the gun in its holster. "I'll do my
best, Pa," he said. "Even if I am as blind as a
bat."

"Talkin' to yourself, kid?"

They had loomed out of the darkness
without a sound like three ghost-riders on
three ghost-horses. Gil gasped in

amazement. "You're here already?" he yelped.

"There's no time better than sunrise, kid," Hornet said.

"I see you got a gun on your hip. You aimin' to use it?"

"If I need to."

"Then use it now ..."

In a panic, Gil fumbled for his gun. He lost his grip before it had cleared the holster.

The gun fell with a thud into the dust at his feet. Hornet winked and shook his head. "Now look at that, boys," he said. "This kid just tried to kill us."

"Shall I finish him, boss?"

"Shame not to."

At that moment, the sun rose clear of the hills. It lit up Gil, and the riders under the elm tree, in a rush of colour. Most of all it lit up the rider who had raised his gun.

CRACK!

The shot seemed to split Gil's ear-drums.
He stepped back and nearly fell. But it was
the gunman who had been hit. "My hand's
busted, boss!" he yelled.

"So is your gun," came a cool, clear voice.
"Anyone else want to try their luck?"

"Molly?"

"Your sister?" Hornet snarled.

"Good morning, Mr Hornet. I'm up here on the bluff with Pa's rifle. Did you know he showed me how to shoot?" Still in shock, no-one moved as she squeezed the trigger again.

CRACK!

This time her target was the other rider. The bullet ripped into his saddle-strap. He fell sideways to the ground with one foot still in a stirrup. His horse bolted at once – dragging him helplessly behind it. There was nothing he could do. "Hey," said the rider with the busted hand. "She's a real pro, boss!

She can pick us off one by one, no bother at all. I'm out of here!"

"Wait – "

"Oh, dear, Mr Hornet," Molly called. "You're all alone now. Are you feeling a bit jumpy?"

"You fixin' to kill me, little lady?"

"I'm fixin' to teach you a lesson, Mr Hornet. Don't bother to get out your gun. You're too far away. You'll never hit me."

Then Molly lifted Pa's rifle and took careful aim.

CLICK!

CLICK! CLICK! CLICK!

Hornet sat up in the saddle. His eyes were narrowed to slits.

"Well, don't that beat all," he said. "Pa's rifle's gone and jammed. Let's see what my rifle can do ..."

He took his time as he slid it out of his saddle bag. Molly stood out against the morning sky – the perfect target. The true-born killer was taking his time again. Maybe that was his mistake. Gil had flung himself to the ground. His gun was back in his hand.

CRACK! CRACK! CRACK! CRACK! CRACK!

There were five shots in all ...

All five zipped into the elm tree. No, not the tree itself. Instead, they hit the grey, wispy nest which clogged its branches. The nest exploded like a huge puff-ball. At once, the air was full of nasty, buzzing little critters that sting you over and over again if you make them jumpy. Or if you're nearest to them.

James Elroy Hornet was nearest to them.

"Aaaagh!" he screamed.

Of course, he did his best to beat them off. But no one can beat off critters as nasty as that. It simply adds to their anger. The true-born killer grabbed his horse's reins.

Soon he was heading for the foot hills in a mad, pounding gallop. Gil and Molly could still hear his frantic screeching as he vanished forever into the shadows.

Chapter 8

Pa's Friends

From the bluff, it was easy to see the ranch house. "Have they all come to breakfast?" Gil gasped. "I've never seen the yard so full of people. The whole town seems to be there!"

"I told you they'd help us," said his sister.

"Yes, you did."

"Pa's friends must have come here along
the river. They were ready and waiting for
the bad guys. That showdown on the trail
was a really bad idea, Gil."

"I'm lucky not to be dead."

"Lucky?"

Gil went red. "OK," he said. "Lucky to
have you as a sister, I mean. Thank goodness

you were learning how to shoot while I was learning how to be a doctor."

Molly grinned. "You did some pretty good shooting yourself, Gil. You must have read my mind as well. How did you know I was aiming at the nest in the tree when Pa's gun jammed?"

"I didn't," said Gil.

"What?"

"I was firing at Hornet, sis."

"You mean all five of your shots were –"

"Misses," Gil nodded.

Now they were both grinning. They were still grinning as they rode back to the ranch. Pa's friends gave them a rousing cheer when they trotted into the yard. It rang out so loud and clear, that every hoodlum in the county must have heard it.

Barrington Stoke would like to thank all its readers for commenting on the manuscript before publication and in particular:

Asim Ahmad

William Allardyce

Alick Chadbund

Toni Clifford

Kyle Crawford

Joshua Fletcher

Danielle Green

Gurjinder Grewal

Jatinder Grewal

Thomas Harrison

Ayesha Iqbal

Amaan Khan

Daniella Mann

Stefano Navarra

Stevie Pantelli

Chris Paul

Nathan Richardson

Beverley Sinclair

Helena Rachel Sinclair

Sanjay Daniel Singh

Reggie Swali

Krystal Taylor

Michael Thomas

Clare Twiselton

Margery Twiselton

Carol Williams

Lauren Williams

Julie Wood

Yasmine Wood

Val Woodward

Become a Consultant!

Would you like to give us feedback on our titles before they are published? Contact us at the email address below – we'd love to hear from you!

info@barringtonstoke.co.uk
www.barringtonstoke.co.uk

Great reads – no problem!

Barrington Stoke books are:

Great stories – from thrillers to comedy to horror, and all by the best writers around!

No hassle – fast reads with no boring bits, and a story that doesn't let go of you till the last page.

Short – the perfect size for a fast, fun read.

We use our own font and paper to make it easier to read our books. And we ask teenagers like you, who want a no-hassle read, to check every book before it's published.

That way, we know for sure that every Barrington Stoke book is a great read for everyone.

Check out www.barringtonstoke.co.uk for more info about Barrington Stoke and our books!